The Christmas Doll

written and illustrated by

Wendy Mathis Parker

Holt, Rinehart and Winston   •   *New York*

Library of Congress Cataloging in Publication Data

Parker, Wendy.   The Christmas doll.

Summary: Anxious to meet Santa Claus, a little girl mails herself to him
and then can't get home again.
[1. Stories in rhyme. 2. Santa Claus — Fiction. 3. Christmas stories]
I. Title.   PZ8.3.P182ch   [E]   79-4067   ISBN 0-03-047111-7

For Todd and Lindy

Way on top of the world, as a whirlwind does blow, stands a quaint little cottage drift-bound by snow. In it are housed the most beautiful toys, soon to be owned by good girls and boys. If you could peek through the frost-covered glass, you'd delight to behold busy elves at their task. All the commotion, fuss, and ado might give you a hint; might give you a clue, to the utter importance of each elf's role. For you see, it is Christmas Eve at the North Pole.

"Jimminy Christmas!" exclaims the head elf. "It's time to check every toy on the shelf." So Alfie, in charge, begins his last caper, checking off toys on his great Christmas paper.

"Let's see," he begins. "Do the tinker toys tinker?"
And the reply that he hears is, "Quick as a winker."
"Now then, dear elves, are the soldiers saluting?"
"Yes, they sure are, and the bugles are tooting!"
But when Alfie asks, "Are the dolls wound for walk-
ing?"

The doll elf replies, "B–but this doll is talking!"

"Talking!" Alfie exclaims, clearly in shock. "Why everyone knows walking dolls don't talk! There's no time to fret 'bout this little doll's quirk. Let's get the dolls wound and see if they work."

And so in the confusion as the dolls are all wound, a brand new accordion drops to the ground. The little pianos go plunkety plunk, and the banjos start strumming out clunkety clunk. The elves delight as the dolls dance and twirl, and it looks like the most joyful place in the world! But suddenly from all of this hullabaloo a tiny little voice utters, "Boo hoo." The dancing and music immediately stop, and the sound would have echoed had a pin dropped. The elves search all over to find the sad noise, and soon they discover it's one of the toys.

Alfie asks, "Why are you crying, cute little doll?"

"Because, I can't walk like the others at all."

"Nonsense, my dear, let's not despair. You just need some oiling a bit here and there."

But when she protests it is no use at all; she then explains, "I'm not really a doll."

"Not really a doll! Well what in the world?"

"No," she replies, "I'm just a little girl."

"Why, Jimminy Christmas and bless my soul! What's a little girl doing at the North Pole?"

"Well, I wanted to meet Santa and see where he lives and see where he makes all the toys that he gives. I wrote and I phoned him and when everything failed, I got in a box and had myself mailed. When Santa received me he opened the box and mistook me for a dolly, a dolly that talks. Santa had misplaced his glasses somewhere, so he put me on the shelf with the dolls over there."

Alfie does his best to comfort and pat her. "Now little girl, what on earth is the matter? You've seen Santa, the toys, and your wish has come true. Not every little girl is as lucky as you!"

"Well, I've never been away from home before this. My mommy and daddy and family I miss. What can I do? Oh me oh my oh. I'll never get back to Columbus, Ohio."

"Poor little girl, you're just feeling homesick. We'll think of a way to get you back home quick." The little girl looks doubtful and doesn't believe that she'll ever get home on, of all nights, Christmas Eve.

"I've got the solution!" an elf does exclaim. "We'll send her back the way that she came!"

The elves all rejoice for the mail is the answer.

"But I must interrupt, if only I can, sir. It's Christmas Eve, with the post office closed; there's no mail that comes and no mail that goes." The elves are all saddened with nothing to say. There must be an answer, there must be a way!

"How about sending her home on a jet? See, little girl, there's no need to fret!"

"That's a brilliant idea, but don't you remember? The airport's been snowbound since the first of December. I hate to be dismal about this whole thing, but she may not get home til early next spring."

"Oh, it's no use," the little girl cries. She feels ever so lonesome and has tears in her eyes.

Then Alfie thinks of something that sounds about right. "You'll accompany Santa on his journey tonight!"

But with all great ideas, problems arise, and one of the elves begins to surmise, "If Santa thinks she's a doll, then there's no one among us, could guarantee she'd be left in Columbus. I must agree, it's a wonderful plan, but he might drop her off in Spain or Japan!"

Just as the elves again start to mope, Alfie says, "Elves, let's not give up hope! I have the answer, here up my sleeve! Let's get the sleigh loaded so Santa can leave!" And so in this magical, mysterious air, the little girl's future is in Alfie's kind care.

The elves are about to put the girl in the sleigh, when a grand "Ho ho ho" comes drifting their way. "Merry Christmas, my elves! What a fine Christmas Eve! I see that the sleigh is all set to leave. Now then, my elves, if I can just find my glasses, I'll be off on my way to the good lads and lasses." The elves help Santa look all around, but his glasses it seems are nowhere to be found. "If we don't find my glasses, how can I get started? Every child in the world will be brokenhearted. I would probably leave

China dolls to the Dutch, and the Chinese don't like wooden shoes very much. I can see that little doll, but nothing much past her. I'm afraid this Christmas may be a disaster."

Then without warning the little girl asks, "Why can't I help, Santa, with your big task?"

Santa thinks for a moment the little doll spoke, but Alfie pretends it's a frog in his throat. He covers her mouth with his quick little hand so she'll speak nothing further, thus ruin his plan.

"Santa, if *I* went with you to help with the toys, I'd deliver them all to the right girls and boys."

Santa agrees that with Alfie assisting, what would it matter that his glasses are missing?

"Please load that doll, Alfie," Santa says to remind him. Then the elves see Alfie hide something behind him. So this is Alfie's strategy, the elves realize, to hide

Santa's glasses and go as his eyes. Alfie can now help the little girl home, regardless of where the reindeer would roam.

The reindeer and sleigh fly them high o'er the world, Santa unaware one of his dolls is a girl.

Soon they see windmills all covered with snow, which tells them that Holland is somewhere below. They land the sleigh on a canal full of ice. "Look Alfie, the Dutch children have all been so nice. Notice wooden shoes set out at each door? That means each child deserves toys by the score. You fill the shoes with candy and toys. We must be sure not to make any noise. I'll leave this cute

doll on the doorstep right here; the little girl this is for has been very good this year!" The doll that Santa leaves by the door is really the poor little girl — and what's more, her eyes widen in fright that she might be left here. But Alfie motions to her she has nothing to fear. As soon as Santa returns to the sleigh, Alfie picks up the girl and packs her away. When the sleigh is once more up in flight, Alfie sighs with relief, "My what a fright!"

A miniature village is sighted below, snug by the Alps in blankets of snow. It looks like a train set from Santa's workshop. This Austrian town will be their next stop. "O Tannenbaum" echoes through mountains so lofty as the sleigh touches down ever so softly.

"This is the custom in Austrian towns, to sing by the tree and dance round and round. What a wonderful Christmas for these good girls and boys. We'll leave dollies and soldiers and all kinds of toys." Then Santa lifts the girl from the sleigh. "I could have sworn I'd given this doll away."

When Santa leaves the little girl as his token, Alfie speaks up and says, "This doll is broken!" He elbows the girl whose arm lifts with a jerk.

"Well, we can't leave a doll whose arm doesn't work! Alfie, please put her back in the sleigh, perhaps you can fix her as we go on our way." Off they fly in the star-spangled night, Alfie hoping and praying that things turn out right.

The reindeer are flying o'er the Great China Wall.

Everything below looks ever so small. When the sleigh lands, Alfie notices a change; Christmas in China is definitely strange. The town is alive with fireworks so bright, all bursting and crackling in colorful light. Below all of the gay lights and rumbling, children are dancing and children are tumbling. A unique holiday custom and loved just as much; how unlike Austria, not at all like the Dutch. Santa intends to give them their due, as he unloads his toys and the little girl, too. So Alfie is faced with the problem once more, to get her back in the sleigh as before. He must get her back to Columbus, Ohio. "Santa, she's not a *china* doll, believe me, I know."

"Pardon me, Alfie, but it is no wonder that without my glasses I could make such a blunder. Well, let's load her again, as I have a notion, it's getting about time to fly cross the ocean. The new world is next; we'll start south of the border. The Mexicans' toys are all made to order." So off they fly from the Great China Wall: Alfie, Santa, the little girl, and all. The little girl looks down at the white ocean foam, and she knows that the sleigh is still far from her home.

The reindeer zoom high in a magical trot, then loop back around as though tying a knot. The sleigh stirs up sparkles as they do fly, and the crystals behind them spell words in the sky: "Merry Christmas, Noel, Feliz Navidad," while the little girl's head is starting to nod. All of these memories the girl wishes to keep, but from dreamlike to dreamland, she falls fast asleep. The reindeer prance on in their dazzling flight, from the old to the new world on Christmas Eve night.

The little girl awakes as they begin to descend; the trip

cross the ocean is now near its end. "How curious," she thinks when she sees Mexico, "that the children have Christmas without any snow." But when they fly closer, it is clear as a bell, the spirit of Christmas is here just as well. A piñata full of candy hangs from the ceiling, while the little ones gather all jumping and squealing. One child is blindfolded and given a stick, but to break the piñata is a difficult trick. The little girl peeks out from her seat in the sleigh and yearns to join the children in play. The sight of the candy is too great a temptation, and she leaps from the sleigh without hesitation. The toys are unloaded as the party goes on, and neither Santa nor Alfie notices she's gone. The little girl is delighted, caught up in the fun. She grabs handfuls of candy and eats every last one. But when she looks up, she is unable to find either Santa or Alfie — they've left her behind. Besides filled with candy she is filled with despair. The dream of her home now has gone up in thin air. The children console her and pat her small hand, but not a word that she utters do they understand. It seems such a pity to have come all this way and to lose sight of home for one moment of play. Not shed a tear she is doing her best to, when here again Alfie comes to her rescue.

"Oh Alfie! You're back! My, what a close call!"

"You're right, little girl, the closest of all! We were nearing Ohio when I thought, 'Jimminy Christmas! Something is missing that is normally with us.'"

"Alfie, oh thank you. What on earth did you do to get Santa to turn the sleigh back for you?"

"Well, little girl, I can't take much credit. It was the way Santa heard it, not the way that I said it. I merely said I was chilly, Santa whipped round the sleigh, and we landed back here by that little café. Santa's next door

eating enough for an army, bowl after bowl of chile con carne! So come on little girl, we had better get going, before Santa leaves us *both* without knowing."

The little girl is dizzy and dazed, being passed back and forth. What a relief to be at last flying north. When finally she spots Ohio's big river, her excitement grows, her heart is aquiver. The fenced patches of farmland, as though stitched with thread, look from above like a quilt for a bed.

Christmas in Holland and China are past. They have made it to Columbus, Ohio at last. Of all the places they have flown over tonight, none to the girl matches this homecoming sight. There are windows with candles and doors decked with greens, which even surpasses her best Christmas dreams. The little girl's eyes sparkle with joy at the sight, seeing her street from above in their flight. But amid all the beautiful houses below, one stands in the darkness without any glow. No wreath on its door, no windows are lit, and though it looks like her house, it just couldn't be it. For her family is always first on the street to hang up their evergreens ever so neat. And yet here is a house where hers normally stood, so something is wrong in the right neighborhood. And while the sleigh

circles she looks for some proof that they are now land-
ing on someone else's own roof.

When Alfie bends over to open the sack, there is no
sign of Santa when he turns back. Santa disappears right
down the chimney, and Alfie in shock cries out, "Oh, by
Jimminy! We've lost Santa little girl! What can we do?
This is a disaster! He fell down the flue!"

"But Alfie, you see, it's not a mistake! It's how Santa
enters a house in the States!"

"What a strange Christmas custom," Alfie thinks to himself, "but if Santa can do it, than so can an elf!"

The little girl watches as the elf disappears. She's been all round the world, but this stop now she fears. What ifs and maybes and thoughts are all pending. Will there be after all a bright, happy ending?

First Santa, then Alfie comes down through the smoke, and they stand by the mantel with a sneeze and a choke. Of all the countries they'd been in tonight, each celebrated Christmas with joy and delight. But this home in America, things just aren't the same, "They're not having Christmas," Alfie says. "What a shame."

Santa is astonished, he just can't believe, this is the same place he'd been last Christmas Eve! No lovely ornaments are hung on the tree, in fact, not even a tree does he see! There are no stockings hung to be filled and no sign of cookies or of milk even spilled! None of the tinsel and bells usually out are seen up above, below, or about. Alfie and Santa just look at each other, then spot in the corner a sad father and mother.

"Ho ho! Merry Christmas!" Santa says, full of good cheer. "Why so unhappy this time of the year?"

The mother and father look very dismayed. "We're not having Christmas this year, I'm afraid. Our little girl's

disappeared," the mother explains, "and without her
Christmas just won't be the same. And since our dear
little girl has been missing, there's been no merrymaking
or mistletoe kissing."

Santa says, "I'm so sorry to hear your very sad news.
There's nothing much worse than the Christmas Eve
blues." Then Santa hears footsteps, the stairway

a-creaking. He turns just in time to catch children a-peeking. In those Christmas Eve faces that are normally glad, he sees little mouths frowning and eyes that are sad. Santa wonders, "Now what would they like? A choo-choo, a football, or maybe a bike?" Then he remembers his most favorite of all, that ever so cuddly that cute Christmas doll. He motions for Alfie to go to the sleigh to bring back that cute little doll right away. Nothing can take their little girl's place, but that doll would brighten up anyone's face. When Alfie returns with the girl in his arms, the children and parents sound off like alarms.

"It's Lindy! It's Lindy!" they all shout for joy, but Santa's confused and still thinks she's a toy. They hug her and twirl her and give her a kiss. He expected some smiles but nothing like this! Santa now wonders and pauses in reflection, then bends over the doll for a closer inspection. And sure enough Santa is in for a surprise, for here this doll is a girl in disguise!

"Well, Jimminy Christmas!" Santa says with a smile. "You mean this little doll was a girl all the while?"

"That's right, Santa, I'm the luckiest girl, to see the North Pole and fly round the world. But the best part of all, I really believe, is to be home with my family on this night, Christmas Eve."

"Well, then, my doll, I mean, one of my lasses, all would be perfect, except for my glasses. If I'd kept them on me, where they belong, I'd never have thought you a doll all along."

Then Alfie remembers the last of his plan, to tug Santa's beard with the sleight of his hand. When Santa looks down to see what feels weird, he finds those old glasses stuck right in his beard!

"Well, Jimminy Christmas! Here are my specs!"

And so Alfie's plan is at last a success. He'd arranged to help Santa wherever they roamed and to somehow deliver the little girl home. So now with their job done they are off on their way, to let this family enjoy Christmas Day.

Even without holly or a tree all aglow, a happier Christmas they would all never know. For this family would say the best gift in the world is that their Christmas Doll is really a girl.